CW00857515

MURDER OF THE MAYOR

WADE DALTON AND SAM CATES SHORT
STORIES BOOK 4

JIM RILEY

To the Most Beautiful

You Always Were and Always Will Be

1

"WHAT'S ON THE LINE?" LIONEL ASKED.

"Feels like a dead alligator. It's not pulling back." Roland answered. "Come help me. It must be a ten-footer, for sure."

The two men tugged and pulled until the weight on the end of the alligator line surfaced.

"Oh, my Gawd! It's a body." Lionel exclaimed.

"Not just anybody. That's Justin Cross, the mayor of Kiln. Oh hell, somebody's in trouble."

2

"WADE, WHAT KILLED HIM?" EMILY ROBINSON PEERED over Wade Dalton's shoulder with her fine blue eyes. "He's yours since you're the only Federal Investigator in the Homochitto Forest. Besides, I'm not sure I want any part of this investigation."

"Looks like somebody stabbed him several times. But there are also lots of turtle bites. We're lucky the alligators didn't get to him before Lionel and Roland hooked him."

"Hell, that's the biggest thing those boys have caught all summer. They spend most of their time drinking shine. Makes it real hard to concentrate on finding gators."

Wade laughed. "Makes it hard to find your toes if you drink enough of it. Who was mad at your beloved mayor?"

"How long of a piece of paper do you have? You can start with his wife. At least they're still married, I think. Then his girlfriend. I'm not sure who the latest one is, but the old one was Mary Poche. From what I hear, she finally tired of all of his promises. Then try his business partner. After him, there are the rest of the people in town. He wasn't the most adored mayor we've ever had. He even tried to hit on me and I'm the Chief of Police here in Kiln."

Wade chuckled. "How did he get elected mayor?"

"Did I mention his business partner? The mayor owned the majority share in the only bank in town. Everybody within thirty miles owes his bank money. He wasn't the kind of man to let them forget it either."

Wade helped Emily lift and place the ex-mayor in a body bag and watched her zip it up. The crew from the Medical Examiner's office arrived and picked up the body.

Wade motioned to them. "Keep this under wraps until I notify his wife and business partner. I wouldn't want them to find out from the television station."

"No problem, Wade." One tech answered. "I wouldn't have cared if they never found the body."

3

WADE APPROACHED THE FRONT DOOR OF THE TWO-STORY house sitting on a large lot on the banks of the Homochitto River. This was not part of the job he enjoyed. The door opened after only two knocks.

"Mrs. Cross, I'm Wade Dalton. I don't know if you remember me. I'm the Investigator assigned to the Forest."

"I met you at a Christmas function or maybe it was at the Mardi Gras parade. I don't remember where I've met you, but I know I have."

"Yes, Ma'am. May I come in?"

She led him into an immaculately furnished living room with a beamed cathedral ceiling. The ornate wall coverings rang out with an aura of wealth. Even the flooring came from the finest imported mahogany.

"Mrs. Cross, I'm afraid I have some bad news."

"Please call me Jane. What did my stupid husband do this time? Was it a dead girl or a live boy he got caught with?"

The response caught Wade off-guard. "Uh—neither one, Mrs. Cross. I'm afraid two fishermen found your husband's body in the forest. Someone killed him. We don't know all the details yet."

Jane's hand covered her open mouth.

"Mother of God! You're kidding me."

"No, Ma'am. I'm sorry. Is there someone I can call for you?"

"Oh, goodness no. I guess I shouldn't be surprised. Probably one of his girlfriends. Or one of their husbands. Justin wasn't very discriminating. He didn't let little things like wedding rings, especially ours, impede his conquests."

Wade saw shock on Jane Cross's face, but no tears.

"Do you have any idea with whom he was last having a relationship?"

Jane laughed. "You make it sound singular. With Justin, he did nothing small time. No, he had to have every skirt in Kiln or he wasn't happy. He didn't line them up single file. If he could bed more than one at a time, he was all the happier."

Wade nodded. "It sounds like you and the mayor had an open marriage."

"Open isn't the right word, Wade. We had a sham for a marriage and have had since the day we got married."

"If you don't mind me asking, then why did you stay with him?"

She eyed him closely. "Money. Simply money. We had a pre-nup. If he left me, I got half of everything he owned. If I left him, I got nothing. So we were both trapped in a business relationship and put on airs for everybody as if they cared. The whole town knew what was going on."

"When did you last see Justin?"

Jane poured herself a drink from a canister sitting on the shelf. She motioned toward Wade, but he shook his head.

"Let's see. What is today?"

"Tuesday."

"Then I last saw him Sunday night. He hasn't been home since then."

"That didn't bother you?"

She laughed out loud. "Honey, if that had bothered me, I would have been in the nuthouse by now."

Wade stared directly at her.

"Did you kill him, Jane?"

She continued to laugh. "I wish I could have, but it isn't in me to do something like that. When you find out who did, though, I want to give him a ribbon. He, or I guess it could have been a she, did the world a favor. If they hold the trial in Kiln, there aren't enough people who didn't hate Justin to sit on a jury to convict whoever killed him. And I get everything he owned now, in case you were wondering. Every last penny."

"Where were you when he was killed?"

She looked at him with raised eyebrows. "When was he killed?"

"We aren't entirely sure, Jane."

"Then how the hell do I know where I was when he died?"

Wade looked down at the floor. "I had to ask to see how you would answer."

"So did I pass the test?" She smiled wryly.

Wade nodded and excused himself from the house.

4

"Hi, I'm Laci. I'm Mr. Robichaux's personal assistant. He will see you in a minute. May I get you some coffee while you're waiting?"

"No, thank you. I'm fine. "

"Is there anything else I can do for you?" Several things went through Wade's mind, looking at the attractive figure in the red low-cut dress. Before he could answer, the buzzer on her desk sounded.

"He's ready to see you now. Will you follow me?"

"Gladly." Wade enjoyed watching her walk ahead of him. She led him into a formal office no less ornate than the mayor's house. After motioning for him to sit in one of the leather chairs, she left, closing the heavy door."

"Wade. Good to see you again. How can Forest Bank be of service today?"

"I'm afraid I'm not here on business, Mark. At least not that kind of business."

A frown crossed Mark's face. "Then the only good thing is you're not with the Regulatory Board. What has Justin done now?"

Wade shook his head. "I don't know. But somebody did something to him. They found his body the Homochitto River."

"Holy cow! Justin is dead?"

"Yes, a couple of alligator hunters found him."

"Do you know who killed him?"

"No, not yet."

Mark sat back in his chair and gazed at the decorated ceiling in his office. After several seconds, he turned his focus back to Wade.

"This changes things—dramatically."

"How so?"

"Justin was the majority shareholder. Now I can buy his shares from the estate and I can run the bank the way it's supposed to run."

"Wouldn't his share go to Jane? I was under the impression from her she would inherit all of his estate."

"She gets everything, Wade. Only in the case of the bank, she will get a fair price determined by an independent arbiter for the shares. Justin and I had a mutual agreement to do that because we didn't want to get saddled with each other's wife in case something like this happened."

"Good planning. Was that your idea or his?"

Mark looked at him as though he didn't understand the question for a second or two.

"Oh, I see. It was actually both of ours. And I didn't just dream it up and then kill him if that is what you're thinking. We've had that agreement in place since we bought the bank."

"You don't seem too upset over his death."

"Upset? I'm happy as hell. It was only a matter of time before Justin ruined everything we had here with his shenanigans. I prayed every day that something would stop him before he took the bank down with him. I never dreamed that something would be murder though."

"I never said he was murdered. How did you come to that conclusion, Mark?"

Mark chuckled. "That's easy. Justin had a clean bill of health at his last physical, and there is no one in town that didn't want him dead. My natural assumption is one of his female companions finally had enough and killed him. And you didn't deny it when I asked you who killed him."

Wade nodded. "I'll have to be more careful. Do you know who he was last seeing outside of his marriage?"

"The current fling is, or was with Linda Hebert. She's a teller with us. I won't have to tell you which one. One look and you'll know whom I'm talking about. Justin hired her, and it wasn't for her ability to count money. She can almost put a complete sentence together if your give her enough time."

"Is there a conference room I can use to talk to Miss Hebert privately?"

"Uh. Sure. I'll get Laci to set it up for you and get Linda."

Wade rose and looked around the office while Mark was on the phone with his assistant. He was impressed with the detail of the décor and the way each piece meshed with all the others. The door opened and Laci motioned for him to follow her again. This time, he followed much closer than before.

"What can you tell me about Linda?"

"Only that I don't think she is the type of person who could stab anyone, not even Mr. Cross. She's too nice to even consider it."

Wade shook his head. "You never know what someone will do given the right circumstances."

A tear dropped on Laci's face. "She couldn't and wouldn't no matter what the circumstances. She's my friend."

They reached a small room with a cherry conference table

and six chairs in the middle. One of the most attractive young ladies Wade had ever seen sat in one chair. Laci closed the door after Wade entered the room.

"Linda, I don't believe we've met. I'm Wade Dalton. I'm the Federal Investigator for the Homochitto Forest."

Her hand trembled when she shook his. She remained silent.

"I understand you have been seeing Justin Cross."

Linda shook her head.

"It's not like that. We're just friends. He and I like to talk to each other. His wife has almost abandoned him and he needs someone to talk to."

Wade realized she did not yet know Justin Cross was dead.

"I hate to be the one to tell you, but Mr. Cross has died."

"Wha—that bitch! I knew she would kill him one day."

Linda burst out in deep uncontrolled sobs from deep within her body. The flood of tears forced her mascara to run down her face onto her dress. Wade found a box of tissues on a table in the corner and handed her several. He waited until she calmed a little before continuing.

"How long have you been seeing each other?"

"You know, don't you? It was more than a platonic relationship."

Wade nodded.

"Three months. We've been together three wonderful months. We were planning to spend the rest of our lives together. He was waiting for the right time to tell his wife."

"Do you know if he told her?"

"He was planning on telling her Sunday night. I don't know if he did or not. He's been out of town all this week."

"Have you talked to him since Sunday?"

"No. I assumed he told his wife and was busy working out

the details of the divorce with her. I guess she had other plans." Again the sobs took over Linda's body. "I'm sorry. I can't go on."

She rose and ran out of the conference room.

Laci entered and stood fuming at Wade.

"How could you do that to Linda? I told you she is the sweetest girl on earth."

"I'm sorry, Laci. In my job, I have to ask tough questions now and then."

"Don't you think you've done enough for one day?" Anger clouded the beauty of Laci's face.

"Yes. I've done enough." Wade did not look at her, but looked at the floor. "I found out what I came here to find."

He strode out of the bank and into his truck.

5

Wade approached the brown brick apartment complex with a bit of trepidation. He wasn't sure how a former mistress of Justin Cross would accept the news of his death. The apartment complex was larger than it appeared from the street. Several tenant buildings behind the ones facing the street surrounded a decent-sized swimming pool. There were several outdoor barbecue pits outside the four foot feet surrounding the pool. Overall, it was one of the nicer layouts Wade had seen in Kiln.

When he knocked on the door, the young lady who answered mildly surprised him. She did not appear to be overly attractive, as Wade would have guessed. Instead, she was at least twenty-five pounds overweight and she did not carry the extra pounds well.

"Hello. Whatcha want? If it's about the rent, we're trying to come up with it. I'm late getting paid this month."

"No. It's not about the rent, Miss Poche. I'm Wade Dalton. I'm—"

"I'm not Miss Poche. Whatcha want with her?"

"I need to speak with her."

"What about?"

"I need to speak confidentially with Miss Poche. Is she in?"

"Why do you need to speak to her alone? Is that asshole causing trouble for her again?"

"I'm sorry. I don't know what you're talking about."

"Then you're the only one in town who doesn't."

"Can I come in? I hate to have this conversation out here on the balcony. There's no telling who might overhear us talking."

"Ha. You don't live in an apartment, do you?"

"No. I don't. Why?"

"Because people on each side of you, above you and below you can hear through these walls. They're thinner than a sheet of onion paper."

"No problem. I really need to talk to Miss Poche. Is she in?"

"Nope."

"Do you know where I might find her?"

"Same place as she always is this time of the day."

Wade shuffled his feet with impatience. Getting information out of this girl was like picking sand out of potato salad on the beach on a windy day. It was one grain at a time.

"Where would that be?"

"At work."

Wade fought the urge to put his hands around the girl's neck.

"Where does she work?"

"In Kiln."

"Do you have an address or the name of the place she works?"

"Yeah, I know where she works."

His fists clenched involuntarily.

"Would you care to tell me where that is?"

"Nope."

The girl slammed the door shut in Wade's face.

6

Wade called Emily on the cell phone number she'd provided earlier in the day.

"Do you have any idea where Mary Poche works? I went by her apartment and she wasn't in."

"Hold on." Wade could hear the sheriff calling to one of the others in the office.

"She's a waitress at the Dempsey's Seafood and Steak. It's probably the best place in town for a steak or fish."

"Great. Do you have an address?"

"Ha. This isn't Evergreen, Wade. Go to the crossroads in town. You can't miss it."

Wade pulled up to the green metal-sided building, surprised at the number of vehicles in the parking lot. He had to park on the edge of the lot and wait in line at the front door. After several minutes, he entered the restaurant. The hostess greeted him with a big smile. Wade took one look at her and knew immediately she was Mary Poche.

"Welcome to Dempsey's. How many will be in your party today?"

"Just me, Mary."

"Make that two." Wade turned to see Emily Robinson standing behind him.

"Sheriff. I'm sorry. I didn't know you were coming."

She smiled. "I thought I would come down and learn how the big city cops do their job."

Wade laughed. "Then you've come to the wrong place. I'm not *big city* by any stretch of the imagination."

"It's all relative, Wade. Compared to Kiln, you're big city. The only time we get any big city guys down here is if our famous quarterback comes home to visit his relatives."

"Oh, yeah. I forgot he is from Kiln. Didn't he move up north?"

"If you call Hattiesburg up north, then you're right."

Wade turned his attention back to the hostess.

"There will be two of us for lunch, please."

"Right this way. We have a table in the back where you might find a little privacy."

When they arrived at the table, Wade pulled out the chair for Emily. After she sat, he circled to the other side of the dining table.

Emily spoke to Mary while Wade was seating himself.

"We really came here to talk to you."

Mary stopped with the menu still in her hand.

"Me?"

"Yes, Hon. We need to talk to you."

"What about?"

"Wade." Emily pointed across the table at him. "He's a Federal Investigator. He has a few questions for you. Can you take a break?"

"Let me check with the manager."

She handed the menu to Wade and scurried to the kitchen area.

"What's good here?" Wade smiled at Emily.

"Everything. From the macaroni and cheese to the T-Bone steaks and everything in between. The shrimp poboy and the fried oysters are great."

Wade looked up at the waitress standing by the table. "I'll have the filet, medium rare, with a baked potato."

Emily glanced up. "I'll have the same."

"So what really brought you down here, Emily?"

"Mark called me from the bank. Any time a majority partner in a financial institution suddenly passes away or quits, it triggers an immediate audit of the books."

Wade studied her expression across the table.

"From the way you look, I'm guessing they found a few discrepancies."

"More than a few. Seems like Justin couldn't support his lifestyle and Jane's lifestyle on the money he was bringing in from his salary at the bank."

"But wasn't he the mayor? That has to pay pretty well."

Emily started laughing. "You are kidding, right? Please tell me you're kidding."

Wade face flushed. "No. I wasn't kidding. I assumed the mayor made good money."

"Wade, this is Kiln. The job of mayor is part time. You couldn't feed an orphan for a week on what we pay the mayor here. Not even a skinny one."

"So why would anyone want the job?"

Emily was still laughing.

"Power. In Kiln, the mayor controls who gets building permits, who gets business licenses and almost everything else. The only other job in the whole county that comes close is the president of the bank. Justin held both positions."

Wade whistled softly. "So he basically controlled Kiln."

"Not basically. He absolutely controlled Kiln and every business in it."

Wade was about to speak when Mary sat down in the chair next to him. She looked at Emily.

"What is this all about? I can't talk long. I have to get back to work."

"No problem. Have you heard about Justin yet?"

"Justin Cross?"

Emily nodded.

"No. Should I have heard something?" Mary's face blushed slightly.

Emily cast a glance at Wade before continuing.

"They found Justin's body this morning. He's dead."

Mary's hand covered her mouth. Her eyes became wide as saucers before tears filled them. She grabbed a napkin and dabbed at the corners.

"How?"

"We're not sure yet, Mary. We don't have the Medical Examiner's report yet."

"I don't believe it. Not Justin. Who—?"

"We don't know that either just yet."

"Why? Why would anyone want to kill him?"

"That's what we wanted to talk to you about."

Mary looked around the crowded restaurant.

"Let's go to the owner's office. We can talk there without the whole town hearing us."

Mary led them through the kitchen to a small office at the rear of the building. When they entered, Wade saw a portly man seated behind the desk.

"Emily, what brings you to our restaurant today? Nobody complained about the food again, I hope?"

"No, Leo. I don't see how anyone could ever complain about your food. I was telling Wade it was some of the best on the coast."

"Not some of the best, Emily." Leo Owens beamed. "It's the very best on the coast. Ask anybody."

Emily laughed. "I don't have to. I've tried it and I love it."

"If it's not the food, then what is it?"

Leo looked at Wade and then back to Emily.

"I'm sorry, Leo. This is Wade Dalton. He's a federal investigator and his territory includes the Forest."

"What does that have to do with the restaurant?"

Wade saw Leo's body stiffen.

"Nothing. I only wanted you to know who he is. We need to speak with Mary and your office is the only place we can have a private conversation. May we borrow it for a few minutes?"

Leo's body immediately relaxed.

"Anything to help our local officials. Let me move some of this paperwork out of your way." Leo grabbed a handful of papers from his desk and exited the office.

"Are you okay, Mary?" Emily asked. "You looked a little pale in the restaurant a few minutes ago."

"Yes. It's Justin. I guess I thought he was invincible."

Emily put her arm around Mary. "I'm sorry to be the one to tell you. Are you sure you're okay?"

"Yes. What Justin and I had is gone. It was already gone before today."

"Tell us about your relationship with Justin. Not the details, but the overall."

Mary pulled a napkin from the box on Leo's desk.

"I'm sure it's not too much different from all of Justin's other relationships. I thought he meant what he was telling me, but he was only using me. I realize it now, but at the time nothing could have convinced me we weren't going to spend the rest of our lives together. The only obstacle was his wife.

Or at least that's what I believed was the only obstacle. If I only knew then what I know now."

"It's okay, Mary. Justin fooled a lot of people in his lifetime."

"But he swore to me he loved me and only me. He was so convincing, you know. Justin had a sensitive side. A lot of people never saw it, but he was sweet when he wanted to be."

"Did you break up with him or did he break up with you?"

Mary started sniffling again.

"He broke up with me." She wiped her eyes and then her nose. "For some hussy down at the bank. It wasn't his fault. She threw herself at him. He was too sweet to resist. She told him she needed him. What about me? I needed him too."

"Do you have any idea who might have wanted to harm Justin?"

Mary shook her head. "No. He only tried to help people in town. He devoted his life to helping others and making sure the town grew."

"Did he ever mention any of his dealings at the bank?"

"Seldom. We didn't discuss business much. We were too busy planning our lives together after he got a divorce. I'm sorry. Can I go now? I don't feel so good."

Emily nodded. "We'll call you if we need anything else."

"Will you tell Leo I had to go? I don't want to go back into the restaurant looking like this."

She pointed to her running mascara.

"No problem, Mary. We'll tell him."

Wade and Emily returned to their table in the restaurant. The waitress appeared with their steaks. "These are just off the grill. We switched your order twice so we could get yours fresh."

"Thanks, Kim. Oh, Mary isn't feeling well. She went

home for the day. Will you tell Leo? We didn't see him in the kitchen."

The waitress laughed. "He's out front smoking and watching the pretty girls coming and going. He has a weakness for pretty girls."

Emily nodded knowingly. "Don't all men? You'd think they would learn sometimes in their lives, but I guess they don't want to."

"You're so right. I've been married for almost forty years and Henry still turns his head when a pretty girl walks by. I don't worry about it though. He's too old to do anything but look."

When Kim went back into the kitchen, Emily leaned across the table. Her voice was barely audible in the crowded restaurant.

"What did you think of Mary?"

Wade cut off a piece of his T-Bone before answering. "I think she is or was the ideal candidate for someone like your former mayor to prey on."

"She still loved him. That was obvious."

Wade nodded. "The only problem is he never loved her. He only used her and then discarded her when he found a shiny new toy to play with."

"Do you have a name for that shiny new toy?"

"I forgot. You weren't with me at the bank."

"No. I was following up with the Medical Examiner. What did you find out at the bank?"

"The name of the new toy is Linda Hebert. She's a teller at the bank."

"Did you talk to her?"

"Yeah. She didn't take the news very well either."

Emily shook her head. "What did those girls see in Justin? He really wasn't anything special. He might have been a mule in the sack. I never tried to find out and never wanted to know."

"Power." Wade said between morsels of steak. "Some young ladies, especially the insecure ones, are attracted to power. In Kiln, Justin seems to have had a monopoly on the power."

Emily put her fork down. "I wished they would have talked to me first."

"Me too. You said Mark called about a discrepancy at the bank."

"Yes. He said an account for marketing expenses was way overblown."

"Does Mark think Cross was embezzling money from the bank?"

Emily nodded. "That's the way it looks."

"Would you like to join me to take a look?"

7

WADE AND EMILY WALKED INTO THE BANK TOGETHER and didn't bother to stop by the loan officers by the front doors. They went directly to Mark Robichaux's office. Outside his confines, Laci Long met them with a glare.

"You again?" She snarled. "I thought I told you that you weren't welcome here anymore."

"We're here to see Mark."

"He's busy. I can set an appointment for you. He should be free to see you in six weeks or so."

"That's okay. We'll go on in and see if he has time for us."

Laci stood up. "I can't let you go in there right now."

"Okay. I wouldn't want to upset you."

Wade went around her desk and opened the door to Mark Robichaux's office. When he saw him poring over some papers on his desk, he strode in despite the protests from Laci. Emily was right behind him.

Mark looked up from the papers. "It's okay, Laci. I called Emily."

Laci stared at Wade while leaving the office.

"Ya'll have a seat. I've been looking at the account I called you about, Emily. It's not as bad as I feared it would be."

"How bad is it, Mark?"

"From an initial brush, I'm guessing he took a two hundred thousand from the bank. His estate can cover that with no problem."

"What about the regulators?"

"They'll fuss and make us go through hoops documenting every time anybody goes to the bathroom without writing it down, but what can they do? The guilty guy is already dead, and there's not much they can do about it. We're reporting the discrepancy as soon as I found out about it."

"You don't think Justin was killed over it?"

"No. He and I were the only ones with access to the marketing account and he was the one that was active in it. I haven't looked at it in years. At least he wasn't dipping into the customers' accounts. Then we would have had serious problems."

"Good. We can erase that from a list of the reasons someone wanted him dead."

"Yep. You never told me how he died. Are you free to discuss it?"

Wade's frown turned to a grin from ear to ear.

"Not right now, Mark. But soon, you will know. Very soon."

He grabbed Emily's arm and motioned for them to leave. When they walked by Laci's desk, he could feel her eyes boring a hole in his back.

He didn't crank the truck when they got in, but turned to the sheriff.

"I need to get an arrest warrant. You know the local judges better than I do."

"Okay. Who and what for?"

24

"First degree murder."

"Damn. You don't waste any time, do you? Are you sure?"

"Positive. How long will it take?"

"Not long. I'll get one a deputy to bring it to us."

The deputy arrived in less than twenty minutes with a search warrant in his hand. Emily looked at him warily.

"You'd better be sure about this. If you're wrong, all kinds of things will happen and you don't want to be a part of them."

"I'm sure."

They walked into the bank and went directly to Mark Robichaux's outer offices. Laci looked up and glared at him when she recognized who was causing the disturbance.

"I told you to leave the bank."

"I couldn't, Laci. Not until I finished my business."

"Finish what business?" She hissed.

"Arresting you for the murder of Justin Cross."

"Do what?"

"You murdered Justin Cross. I don't know all the details yet, but I'm certain you killed him."

Her voice became shrill. "How can you come in here and accuse me of such a thing?"

The door to Mark Robichaux's office opened, and Mark stepped into the outer area.

"What's going on?"

Laci glared at Wade. "This idiot is trying to arrest me for Mr. Cross's murder."

Wade glanced at Robichaux before turning his attention back to Laci.

"I'm not trying, Laci. I am arresting you and charging you with first degree murder in the death of Justin Cross."

"On what evidence?"

"Because you told me Linda could not have stabbed

Justin. You couldn't have known he was stabbed unless you were the one who stabbed him."

Laci's eyes widened. "Mr. Robichaux must have told me when he asked me to get Linda."

Wade looked at Mark. "Did you?"

"I—uh, I don't think so, but I could have mentioned the murder investigation to her."

"Think, Mark. Did or did you not tell her?"

He did not look at Laci, but at Wade.

"I probably said something about you looking into Justin's death. I can see where she would assume someone murdered him."

"But you said nothing about him being stabbed, did you?"

"No. I didn't know myself and I forgot to ask how he died."

"Laci, you were very specific in telling me Justin was stabbed. That's why you're under arrest. I'm sure we'll find the corroborating evidence fairly quickly."

The wild look left Laci's face, and she plopped down in her chair. Tears flowed freely down her symmetrical face.

"He was a pig. Linda was in love with him, and he kept trying to screw me. I didn't want to tell her, so I went to talk to him at the dock Monday morning before work. He tried to fondle me while I talked to him. I lost control and picked up an ice pick and stabbed him. I stabbed him over and over. I couldn't stop. When I realized what I had done, he was in a pool of blood on the dock. I pushed his into the river and went home, showered, and changed clothes before I came to work."

Wade nodded. "I assumed it was something like that."

She looked at Mark Robichaux.

"I'm not sorry I did it."

NOTES

Murder of the Mayor is Wade Dalton and Sam Cates short story. It features the dynamic duo with even greater challenges.

I have taken great literary license with the geography and data of south Mississippi. They are wonderful and a great way to experience the deep South culture. I lived there for over five years and found it to be one of the most desirable places on earth if you enjoy the outdoors, great cuisine and remarkable people.

There are so many people to thank:

My family, Linda, Josh, Dalton & Jade

David and Sara Sue

C D and Debbie Smith

My brother and sister-in-law, Bill & Pam

My sister, Debbie

My sister-in-law and her husband, Brenda & Jerry

The Sunday School class at Zoar Baptists

Any and all mistakes, typos and errors are my fault and mine alone. If you would like to get in touch with me, go to my web site at http://jimrileyweb.wix.com/jimrileybooks.

I thank you for reading **Murder of the Mayor** and hope you will also enjoy the rest my books.

Dear reader,

We hope you enjoyed reading *Murder of the Mayor*. Please take a moment to leave a review, even if it's a short one. Your opinion is important to us.

Discover more books by Jim Riley at

https://www.nextchapter.pub/authors/jim-riley

Want to know when one of our books is free or discounted? Join the newsletter at

http://eepurl.com/bqqB3H

Best regards,

Jim Riley and the Next Chapter Team

Lightning Source UK Ltd.
Milton Keynes UK
UKHW021900010321
379622UK00012B/1129/J